We Were Never Meant to Be

Betrayal is the most dangerous thing out there...

ARYAMAAN YADAV

Made with ❤ on the Notion Press Platform

www.notionpress.com

Contents

Prologue

CONFIDENTIAL REPORT

Case ID: #472-BH

Filed By: Officer Thomas Johnson

Department: Forest Division – Black Hollow Region
Date: October 12th

Subject: Missing Persons – Black Hollow Trail

On the morning of October 10th, a group of six teenagers—identified as Jack Reynolds, Emma Carter, Liam Brooks, Chloe Mitchell, Sophie Turner, Tom Smith and one unnamed local guide—entered the restricted forest zone near Black Hollow Trail for a five-day hike. They were last seen by a shopkeeper at the trail entrance around 9:14 a.m.

 One week later, an SOS call was received from an unknown number, consisting of static, fragments of screaming, and the words: "They're gone... He is ..." The signal was lost immediately after.

Search operations began within 9 hours. Initial findings revealed torn fabric, scattered belongings, and blood traces near the river bend. No bodies were recovered—except for one.

The sole survivor, Sophie Turner, was found 36 hours later near a camp, in shock and suffering from severe dehydration and memory trauma. Before collapsing, she whispered a single sentence:

"He was not what he seemed to be…"

The case remains under active investigation. Locals believe this to be the third unsolved disappearance in the region in recent years. As of this writing, the Black Hollow Trail remains closed to the public until further notice.

1. Silence Before the Storm

It was a beautiful morning -- until my friends knocked on the door and ruined the silence. I woke up groggy and confused, only to find them already geared up for the trekking trip I had completely forgotten about. While they laughed at my panic, I rushed to pack my bag — a torch, some food, and my phone. Jack, always the planner, reminded everyone to leave their phones behind. *"It ruins the experience,"* he said. I nodded, then quietly slipped mine into my backpack anyway. Just in case something went wrong.

We took the bus to the trekking site — strangely empty, like no one else wanted to go there. I sat next to Emma, who leaned in and whispered, "Sophie, this place is kind of famous... lots of people have gone missing here."

I rolled my eyes. Emma loved telling creepy stories just to mess with us, and I was not falling for it. I cracked open the window, and a cool breeze slipped in, brushing through my tangled hair like a silent warning I chose to ignore.

The bus came to a screeching halt near a rusty signboard half-covered in moss. *"Ridge Trail,"* it read, barely legible through the dirty window. The driver did not even wait for us to unload -- he just nodded once and pulled away like he could not leave fast enough. *"Well, that wasn't weird at all,"* Emma said sarcastically, adjusting her backpack. We stood in silence for a moment. No birds. No cars. No sound, except the crunch of gravel beneath our boots as we walked past the sign.

The trail curved into dense forest almost immediately, replacing the sunlight with shadows. Jack took the lead, as usual, with Emma and I close behind. *"Do you guys hear that?"* Liam asked suddenly, hugging his jacket closer. *"It's like… someone is pulling us down."* I felt it too, but we just laughed at it like nothing. Maybe it was the cold. Maybe it was something else.

We kept walking for hours — what felt like days. Just as we were about to stop and catch our breath, something in the corner of my eye caught my attention.

A tree.

Unlike the others — pale, almost ghostlike, its bark bone-white against the shadows. I stepped off the trail and moved toward it, drawn in by something I could not explain. Etched into the trunk, in jagged letters, were the words:

Black Hollow Trail.

I turned to call the others, but before a word left my mouth, a sharp chill slid down my spine. My body froze. It was like time itself had stopped — I could not move, could not breathe. And then I saw it. Something — or someone — strode silently past me, just out of sight. Not running. Not rushing. Just... moving, like it belonged here, and I did not.

My breath hitched. I spun around, but the figure had already disappeared into the trees. No footsteps. No rustling. Just silence — thick, pressing silence. My heart pounded against my lungs like it wanted to escape. Maybe I imagined it. Maybe I was just tired. But my instincts told me otherwise.

I rejoined the group, saying nothing. Liam cracked a joke about getting lost, and Tom laughed, but I could not shake the feeling that we were not alone. As we moved deeper into the forest, the trees seemed to close in behind us, swallowing the trail — and the uneasy truth I had not told anyone yet.

Something was already watching.

2. The Guide

I tried to shake off the uneasy feeling and had just started walking with the group again when we all heard something.

"That's far enough," a voice called out from the trees.

We all froze.

A man stepped into view, tall and lean, wearing a worn green jacket and boots caked with dried mud. His face was calm, unreadable. *"You must be the group I was told about,"* he said. Jack stepped forward. *"Are you... the guide?"* The man nodded. *"Name's Logan. I know these woods better than the back of my hand."*

His eyes briefly met mine, and for a second, I felt the same chill I had felt back at the white tree. But he smiled politely and added, *"Let us get moving. The sun does not wait."*

Logan led us deeper into the trail with practiced steps, as if he had walked it a hundred times. His boots made no sound on the dead leaves beneath us — something I only noticed after Tom whispered, *"Is he even making a sound?"*

We laughed it off, of course. It was probably the forest playing tricks on us. Still, I started to walk a little closer to Jack.

Logan talked as we walked — stories about past trekkers, missing people, and strange legends. His voice had a strange calmness, like someone telling a bedtime story... only, these were not the kind you would want to hear before sleeping.

"There was a group once," he said, *"five, just like you."* Came through here a few years ago. Never made it back." We stopped walking. He turned to look at us, smiling like it was just a joke. *"Kidding,"* he said. *"Mostly."* I should have laughed. I should have said something smart back. But the way he looked at me — not like he was amused, but like he was waiting for a reaction — made the words fade in my throat.

As we walked, the trees grew closer, darker. Sunlight barely reached the forest floor now. Emma muttered something about *"classic horror movie vibes,"* but nobody laughed this time.

Chloe had not said a word since we left the bus. Not even a nod. I nudged her gently. *"You okay?"*

She glanced at me, then quickly looked away. Her lips were pressed into a tight line. Maybe she was tired. Maybe she did not like Logan. Maybe both.

Tom tried to lighten the mood. *"So, Logan, you live around here?"*

"Born and raised," he replied.

"Though not many of us stay. People either leave... or disappear."

That smile again. Jack rolled his eyes. *"You are really leaning into the whole creepy-woods-guide thing."* Logan looked back at Jack. *"I do not have to lean into it, son. These woods are old. They remember everything."* That shut us up.

We kept walking. The trail narrowed, and the forest swallowed us whole. It felt like no matter how far we walked; we were not getting anywhere. The path twisted in on itself, like it was playing a game we did not know the rules to. I kept glancing over my shoulder. Nothing. Just trees. But it felt like... something was watching.

Logan stopped suddenly, crouching beside a mossy rock. *"What is it?"* Liam asked. Logan did not answer. He ran his fingers across the bark of a nearby tree — deep slashes were carved into it. Claw marks? *"Bear?"*

Jack asked, keeping his distance. Logan tilted his head. *"Could be. Or not."*

"Could you be less creepy?" Tom muttered, half-joking, but we all noticed the way he moved closer to the group. Emma fidgeted with her backpack strap. *"I thought this was supposed to be a popular trail?"* Logan stood. *"It was. Once."*

Night fell earlier than expected. Too early. The sky dimmed, and a strange feeling hung over everything. No birds. No wind. Just... silence.

"Let's set up camp," Logan said. *"You would not want to be walking in this forest after dark."* We did not argue. We made a small fire. It crackled and hissed, but the light did not feel warm. It felt like a spotlight on prey.

I sat beside Chloe again. She hugged her knees to her chest, her eyes locked on the fire. She did not say anything — not even when I gently nudged her shoulder. She just stared. Not at the flames, but at Logan.

Her face was unreadable, like she knew something none of us did... or maybe she was just scared. But the way she did not blink — the way her breath stayed so steady — it made me feel like I should be scared too.

"You kids get some sleep," he said softly. "Long walk ahead tomorrow." He walked off into the trees without another word.

As I curled deeper into my sleeping bag, the firelight flickering behind my eyelids, sleep started to pull me under. My thoughts drifted — the trek, Liam, Emma's story, Logan's unreadable stare.

But just before sleep took me completely, I saw something.

A shadow moving.

Liam. Maybe Tom. Could also be Jack.

Stepping away from the campfire, into the dark woods. And behind him... a taller figure, walking silently beside him.
One I did not recognize.

I was too tired to think. Maybe I was dreaming.
I closed my eyes.

3. Lost Signal

The morning was perfect.

Birds chirped above us, the sun shined golden light through the trees, and for a moment, it almost felt like an ordinary camping trip. Jack and Tom were arguing over who made the worse instant noodles, like old times. Emma was brushing her hair, humming softly. Logan handed out energy bars with a friendly smile, like some wilderness camp counsellor. Even Chloe looked… calmer, sitting cross-legged with her journal.

I stretched, yawned, and took a deep breath of the cool forest air. *"Not bad, right?"* I said to no one in particular.

That is when I noticed.

Liam was gone.

His sleeping bag was still zipped up, but empty. His bag sat untouched beside it, and the cereal he told he was going to eat was still there. No note. No footprints. No Liam.

Jack was the first to notice me standing still.
"What's up?" he asked, mouth half-full of dry noodles.
"Where's Liam?" I asked quietly. That question froze everyone. Emma's hum stopped. Tom dropped his fork. Chloe did not move.

"What do you mean?" Jack said, but his voice was already tight. *"He's not here,"* I said. *"His stuff is still there, but he's not."* Emma stood up, looking around wildly. *"Liam? Hey—Liam, quit messing with us!"*

No answer.

We all scattered wildly, searching the nearby trees and bushes, calling his name. Jack pushed into the woods a few feet, yelling louder each time. Tom checked behind the rocks near the stream. Emma circled the camp three times before finally sitting onto a log, shaking.

"I saw him last night," she said. *"He was right there, laughing at Jack's dumb story."*

"And no one had seen him leave." Jack said.

I hesitated to talk about what I had saw last night, doubting if it was even real or just a dream manifested by my subconscious mind.

Logan did not say anything for a moment. Then, with a calmness that felt too rehearsed, he stood up and clapped his hands together.

"Alright," he said. *"Everyone stop. We need to stay calm."*

"But he's gone," Jack snapped. *"He wouldn't just leave!"*

"We don't know that," Logan said smoothly. *"Maybe he went to explore or take a walk. Maybe he just needed a break."*

"He left all his stuff," I said. *"Even his snacks."*

Logan looked at me, then nodded slowly. *"Then we will find him. But not like this — panicking and splitting up will only make things worse."*

He gathered us around like a teacher calming a class trip. *"Here is what we will do. Stick together. Follow the path near the clearing. I will lead. Jack, you take the rear. We will circle back to this spot in an hour. Got it?"* No one objected, but no one really agreed either. We just… followed. And deep down, I think we all knew — Liam had not *gone* anywhere.

He had vanished.

As we walked, the silence between us grew louder. Every snapped twig made me flinch. Emma kept glancing over her shoulder, her hands fidgeting with her braid until it became completely messy. Jack muttered words under his breath, kicking at rocks like it would bring Liam back. Chloe, of course, remained silent — but her steps were slower, her eyes scanning the trees like she was expecting something to leap out. Tom kept looking at trees and the surrounding area, as if Liam would jump out of them.

No one was talking about it, but we were all thinking the same thing: Liam would not have just left. Liam would not just leave his stuff.

After half an hour of walking in looping trails, we ended up right where we started. Jack ran his hand through his hair and let out a frustrated groan. *"This is stupid,"* he said. *"We are going in circles! Why isn't he answering?!"*

Emma looked at the ground. *"He did not even take his phone. None of us did… except maybe —"*

I quickly looked away before anyone could notice. I had my phone. It was buried deep in my bag, still turned off. I was not supposed to bring it. I could feel the weight of it like a secret sinking in my pocket.

Logan clapped his hands once, sharp and commanding. *"We'll search again later,"* he said. *"Right now, we stay put. The forest can play tricks on you. Do not let it."*

But the tricks had already started.
And one of us was already gone.

That night, no one spoke much around the fire. The usual jokes and laughter were replaced by long stares and whispered doubts. Tom tried to stay upbeat as always, cracking a joke about Liam pranking us, but his voice broke halfway through. No one laughed. I sat curled in my sleeping bag, eyes locked on the flickering flames, pretending not to hear Jack quietly sobbing behind a tree. And even though Logan said he would keep an eye on the surroundings, I caught him staring into the woods — not with fear, but with something else. Something unreadable.

4. Echoes

The forest felt colder that morning.

No one said it out loud, but something had shifted. The forest was not quiet anymore. It listened. Every snapped twig echoed too long, and the birds had stopped singing. Even Jack's voice, usually loud, came out in a whisper. Like he did not want something to hear. Emma kept pacing. Tom clutched a small branch like a weapon. And Chloe… well, Chloe was silent as ever.

Liam had not yet returned. We decide to split up slightly for a moment in a last effort to find Liam. Jack went next to the stream. Tom circled around the camp. Emma went to check a nearby trail. I, for no specific reason, go to the white tree, in hopes that it had attracted Liam the same way it had attracted me. Chloe just sat next to the fire, writing something in her journal, observing the surrounding area. I do not find anything at the white tree, so I go on to check on Emma with Tom.

We go deep into the abandoned trail, but find no sign of her.

"Emma?" I frantically shout.
Silence.

"Guys, she was just here! She was literally just here!" Tom shouted, voice breaking.

The forest had never felt so vast. My heartbeat pounded in my ears as they all called out Emma's name again and again, but the trees just swallowed the sound like a secret. No reply. No rustle. Not even birdsong. It was as if Emma had never been there. As if the woods had taken her — quietly, efficiently, like it had done this before.

Logan raised both hands, voice low but steady. *"Everyone stay close. She could not have gone far. Let us not panic."*
But it was too late for that.

Jack kicked a rock in frustration. *"This cannot be happening again. First Liam, now Emma?"*
Tom mumbled something about heading back, but no one moved. They just stood there; eyes locked between the trees like they expected something—*someone*—to step out.

I turned away for a moment, trying to breathe. That is when I saw it—half-hidden behind a bush, tied to a low branch.
Emma's scarf. Twisted into a loose knot. Too clean. Too deliberate.

I did not say anything right away. Just stared. It did not look dropped or torn—it looked *placed*. No signs of struggle.

"Guys..." I called, her voice trembling. *"Look."*
She stepped aside so they could see it — the scarf, fluttering faintly in the breeze like it was waving *goodbye*.
Jack's face went pale. *"That is Emma's. No way she left it like that."*
Tom shook his head slowly. *"Then who did?"*
Everyone looked at Logan.
He did not flinch. *"Maybe she marked her way back. Let us not jump to conclusions."*
But Sophie was not convinced. That scarf had not been there before. And the knot—it was tied *too perfectly*.

The camp was quiet—too quiet. Even the insects seemed to be holding their breath. I sat near the dying sparks of the fire, arms wrapped around my knees. The group had barely spoken since Emma vanished. Chloe had not said a word, as always. Tom was staring into space. Jack paced restlessly, whispering things under his breath. And Logan...
Logan had gone off alone, saying he needed to *"clear his head."* That was hours ago. I finally crawled into

her tent, but sleep felt impossible. Her thoughts twisted and turned like the shadows outside.

That night, long after the fire had died and the others had fallen into uneasy sleep, I lay wide-eyed in my tent. The silence was too thick, pressing on my chest like something sitting on my lungs. And then—I heard it. Faint, carried by the wind.
"Sophie..."
My breath stopped.
"Sophie... come here..."
It was Emma's voice.
Soft. Familiar.
Coming from the woods.
But something in the way it echoed felt wrong—*off*, like it was stitched together from memory.

It just felt too real.

Surreal.

I did not move. I just clutched my sleeping bag tighter, eyes locked in the darkness. I did not sleep that night.

5. Cracks

The forest was colder than before.

We did not talk much that morning. Jack lit a small fire with shaking hands, while Chloe just sat—staring at the flames, like they might whisper answers if she stared long enough. No one had slept. I do not think any of us *could* sleep, not after Emma vanished like Liam did.

Tom kept pacing. *"She's not gone,"* he muttered. *"She is just… hiding. Maybe playing a joke. This is all just one sick game, right?"*

Nobody answered him.

Then Jack stood up and snapped, *"Open your eyes, Tom! Emma's gone. Liam's gone. And the only thing connecting all of this is that stupid trail and him."* He pointed straight at Logan.

Logan did not even flinch. He just stood by the edge of the trees, hands in his pockets, eyes scanning the woods. *"I told you already,"* he said quietly. *"I do not know what is happening. I have hiked here for years. This… this is not normal."*

"That's exactly what makes it suspicious," Jack snapped. *"Why are you so calm, huh? You were the one who said no phones. You led us here."*

Logan raised his hands. *"Because panicking will not help. I am trying to keep everyone alive."*

Alive.

That word hung in the air like smoke—thick and choking.

I looked around. Chloe was still quiet, but something in her face had changed. She looked... almost afraid. But not of Logan. Of something else. Of *us*.

Tom stepped in between Jack and Logan, his voice rising. *"What are you saying, Jack? That he took them? That Logan—what, dragged them into the woods while we slept? That is insane!"*

Jack's eyes were bloodshot. *"Is it? Tell me, how does someone vanish without a sound? Twice?"*

"He's the guide," Tom said. *"He knows the area. He is trying to help."*

Jack shoved Tom. *"Stop defending him! You think this is normal? You think we are all just going to walk out of here fine if we follow Logan like good little sheep?"*

"Maybe if we don't start fighting each other," Tom snapped. "We can get out of this alive!"

A stick cracked beneath someone's boot. Everyone froze.

Logan spoke, voice like gravel: *"Yelling won't bring anyone back."*

Jack pointed again, his hand trembling. *"Then tell me why you were up before any of us. Just standing there."*

"I was checking the perimeter," Logan said coolly. *"We're not alone out here."*

That shut everyone up.

Even Tom looked shaken. I glanced at Chloe—still silent. Still watching. But now her fingers gripped the edge of her jacket tightly, like something inside her was trying to crawl out.

Jack stormed off toward the trees, but not too far. *"I am done listening to him. From now on, we make decisions together. No more following Logan."*

For the first time, Logan smiled—but it did not reach his eyes.

"Of course," he said softly. *"Whatever makes you... feel safer."*

Tom looked between Jack and Logan, torn. *"We shouldn't split,"* he said finally. *"But... Jack's right. From now on, we decide what happens."*

I nodded slowly, heart pounding. *"Agreed."*

Emma and Liam were gone. Trust was crumbling. And Logan... Logan seemed untouched by it all.

Chloe did not speak, but for the first time in days, she moved—stood up, brushed herself off, and walked away from the group to sit beneath a tree, alone. Her silence was no longer natural. It felt deliberate.

Logan's gaze followed her for a second too long before turning back to the fire.

Jack sat with his arms crossed, his back turned to all of us. Tom muttered something to himself and began carving into the dirt with a stick—anything to distract from the suffocating quiet that followed.

None of us said it aloud, but the truth was there, sitting with us like a shadow:

We were breaking.

6. The Silent One

The morning was colder than any before it. The kind of cold that crept under your skin, not because of the weather — but because something was *wrong*. No birdsong, no breeze, just silence, thick and uninterrupted. The fire had long died, and none of us had the energy to relight it.

Chloe was already awake, sitting cross-legged near the edge of the camp. Her back was to us, her head tilted slightly as if she were listening to something far away. She had not said a word since the trip began — but now her silence felt heavier. Intentional. Like she was hiding something in it.

Tom looked around and muttered, *"Where's Jack?"*

That was when I noticed the missing backpack. The scuffed boots. The empty space beside the fire.

Jack was gone.

And Chloe, finally turning her head toward me, whispered a single line that sent a chill down my spine:

"He shouldn't have gone looking for the truth."

Tom stood up immediately. *"What do you mean by that?"* he snapped, walking over to Chloe.

She did not answer. Just stared at the place Jack had slept, her expression unreadable. The shadows under her eyes looked deeper this morning, as if she had not slept at all.

"Chloe," I said, softly but firmly. *"Did you see something?"*

She turned to me slowly. Her lips moved — barely. *"He asked questions. The kind you are not supposed to ask here."*

"What does that even mean?" Tom asked. *"What the hell is going on with you?"*

Chloe flinched, but did not speak again.

Logan approached, calmer than anyone had ever been. *"Let's not jump to conclusions,"* he said, voice steady. *"Maybe Jack just... went to cool off. We all know how short-tempered he can be."*

Tom glared. *"Without his bag? Without telling anyone?"*

"I'll look for him," Logan offered. *"Alone. I know these woods better than anyone."*

"No," I said quickly, surprising even myself. *"We stick together now. No more splitting up."*

Logan gave a half-smile. *"Of course. Just trying to help."*

But I saw it. A flicker. Just for a moment — something behind his eyes. *Satisfaction?*

We called for Jack for hours. No reply. No trail. No footprints.

And by nightfall, when we finally gave up and sat back down in the cold, Chloe spoke again.

"They're not lost. They are being taken."

We sat around the diminishing fire, the silence between us more suffocating than the cold. No one wanted to sleep. No one wanted to speak. The shadows cast by the flames stretched long and distorted across the trees.

"I'm not closing my eyes," Tom muttered. *"Not until I know what the hell is going on. One by one? Seriously?"*

His voice cracked slightly at the end. He tried to act tough, but I could see it in his trembling hands — fear.

Chloe had curled into herself, arms wrapped tightly around her knees. Her lips moved now and then, soundless. Like she was whispering to something only she could hear. I wanted to ask her what she was saying, but something about the way her eyes locked into the darkness told me not to.

Logan poked the fire with a stick, casually. *"Panic never helps,"* he said. *"All we can do is rest and move early. Panicking only gets people hurt."*

Tom shot him a look. *"So does trusting the wrong people."*

I stared into the fire, pretending it could take away the unease spreading through my body. My mind kept replaying Liam walking into the woods. Emma's otherworldly whispers. Jack's sudden absence. And Chloe... still silent, still trembling, as if she knew what was coming next. Everyone was unravelling — including me. But what scared me most was not the disappearances. It was how *normal* Logan seemed. Calm. Collected. Like he already knew the ending.

I laid down beside Emma's now-empty sleeping bag, trying to calm my twisted thoughts. The forest was too quiet — no rustling leaves, no crickets, just the soft crackle of the dying fire. Every time I closed my eyes; I saw shadows moving behind my eyelids. My heart would not slow down. I clutched my bag closer, pretending it was for warmth, but really... I just needed to hold onto *something*. I told myself I was safe. But my mind did not believe it.

Just as I began to drift into uneasy sleep, I heard the unmistakable sound of footsteps... but *no one was supposed to be awake.*

7. All That's Left

The morning was dull and grey, as if the sky itself had given up. It hung heavy above the forest, thick with a silence that did not feel natural. I opened my eyes, hoping last night had been a nightmare, but Tom's place was empty. Again. His backpack still sat where he left it, untouched. Panic did not hit me instantly this time. It came slowly, like a slow chill creeping over me, because by now, I knew exactly what this meant.

Logan stood up and clapped his hands together. *"Pack your things. We need to move."*
"No," I said quietly, my voice cracking. *"We can't just keep walking like everything's fine."*
Liam, Emma and Jack were already gone. Now Tom. The silence around us was loud, like the trees were listening.
Then Chloe — who had barely spoken the entire trip — looked straight at me. Her voice, when it came, was low and steady.
"We are not lost. We are being hunted."

I stared at Chloe, heart pounding. Her eyes did not blink.
Before I could respond, she turned sharply, like she had heard something.

"Did you hear that?" she whispered.

I strained to listen — nothing but the rustle of wind through dry leaves.

Then it happened.

A sharp movement. A shadow from the trees. Chloe did not even scream.
I watched, frozen, as something — someone — dragged her back into the woods. Her hand reached out to me for just a second before it vanished in the dark.

And her voice echoed. Not in the air — in my head.
"The voices lie. You lie."

I could not move. My feet were planted, my breath stopped in my throat.
She was just there. Speaking. Alive.

And then... gone.

I stumbled back, eyes wide, heart slamming against my chest. *"No, no, no—"*
Logan grabbed my arm. *"We must go. Now."*
I jerked away from him. "You did not see that?! You did not even try to help!"

He did not answer. His face was calm — too calm.

I dropped to my knees, the cold earth digging into me.
The silence roared louder than ever.
My thoughts spiralled.
Chloe's words clung to me like glue:
The voices lie. You lie.

I looked up. Logan was already walking away.

I walked. I do not know for how long. My legs moved on their own, numb and trembling.

Every crunch of leaves beneath my feet echoed louder than it should have.
I was alone. Not just physically — deeply, painfully alone.

Liam. Emma. Jack. Tom. Chloe. All gone.
Because of me?

If I had told them about the shadow I saw that night — when Liam disappeared...
If I had stayed closer to Emma, if *I had stopped* Jack from wandering off...
If I had woken up when I heard Tom's footsteps...

If I had listened to Chloe when she spoke, finally spoke...

They were warning signs.
And I ignored every single one.

This was not just a bad trip. It was a curse. And I had cursed it.

My phone, deep in my bag, felt like a lifeline I was too scared to reach for.

What would I even say?

"Hi, I'm the girl who *doomed her friends*."

The words echoed in my mind:

The voices lie. *I lie.*

I sat on a damp rock, staring into the blackness ahead. The forest was still now. Like it had gotten what it wanted.

I whispered their names to the trees.

But the wind did not answer.

Only the shadows did.

And one of them…

was walking toward me.

The forest was still.

My shoes crunched through the ground as I stumbled toward Chloe—too late. Her motionless form lay beneath the ghost-white tree, eyes wide open, lips as if her last breath had frozen mid-plea.

Behind me, Logan emerged slowly, like a shadow peeling away from the trees.

"*I warned her,*" he said softly, "*but some people don't listen.*"

I turned, my face pale but eyes burning. "*You did this.*"

He smiled. "*You were all so easy to read. Jack with his hero act. Liam, always distracted. Emma, desperate to believe in anything. And Chloe... well, she knew something was wrong. That made her dangerous.*"

I took a shaky step back. My heart pounded. "*You brought us here. You watched us fall apart. Why?*"

Logan shrugged. "*People always show who they truly are when they are scared. I just... gave fear a little push.*"

My gaze landed on a thick tree branch on the ground—broken, pointed.

"*You think I'm scared of you?*" I said, voice trembling.

"*You're scared of yourself,*" he whispered. "*You followed. You doubted. You froze. You were the easiest one to turn.*"

"*No.*" I reached for the branch. "*Not anymore.*"

I swung—desperate, focused. It hit him hard across the chest, knocking the wind out of him. He staggered back, stunned.

"You don't get to win," I said.

He looked at me one last time, breath shallow, shocked that I had fought back. Then he collapsed.

Silence.

I dropped the branch. The woods around were empty now—except for the whispers of the wind and my own heartbeat.

I knelt beside Chloe, brushing dirt from her face.

"I'm sorry," I whispered. "You were right."

I stood, alone.

But not broken.

Epilogue: His Words

The recorder was cold in my hand — a dull, grey thing tucked inside Logan's bag. I almost did not see it. I almost did not care.

It was labelled, in a faded handwriting:

For The One Who Survived.

But something told me to press play.

Click.
A burst of static. Then... his voice.

Calm. Too calm.

"If you are listening to this... congratulations. You lived. The odds were never in your favor, but something in you...survived."

I froze. My breath stopped in my lungs.

"They came here thinking it was just a trail. Just another pretty place to escape the noise. But noise finds you — even in silence. Especially in silence."

My fingers clenched the device.

"Each of them carried something heavy. Secrets. Regrets. Guilt. And guilt... guilt is the easiest thing to feed. All it takes is a whisper."

I wanted to scream. To throw the recorder into the fire. But I could not stop listening.

"I did not make them vanish. Not really. I just showed them the path to walk. They all believed me, because no one ever suspects the guide. One by one. And they walked it. Willingly. It is fascinating how fear does more damage than knives ever could."

I shut my eyes. Jack. Emma. Tom. Chloe. Liam. Their names echoed in my head.

"You think I am a monster. Maybe I am. But monsters do not hide in shadows anymore. They hike beside you. Laugh with you. Tell you ghost stories by the fire. Until the story becomes your reality."

I could almost see him saying it — the twisted smile, the unblinking eyes.

"They were never meant to last. None of you were. Some bonds are just... never meant to be."

Click.

And that was it.

Just silence.

No tears came. Not yet. Only the sound of the wind in the trees — like whispers that never stopped.